The Forest of Friendship by Sitala Peek

Illustrations by Simon Lucas

First Published in Great Britain in 2023 by Beercott Books,
Kineton, Warwickshire, United Kingdom.

ISBN 978-1-7393020-0-9

A CIP catalogue record of this book is available from the British Library.

Beercott

Sitala Peek

The Forest
of
Friendship

Illustrated by Simon Lucas

A young tree stretched in the morning sun and happily wriggled his roots deeper into the ground.

The forest was beginning to stir.

But something was wrong.

A squirrel ran up the trunk of the little tree, sniffed the air, and squealed.

The little pine could smell it too - the bitter smell of smoke.

And smoke meant fire.

Like all trees, he had a deep fear of large fires.

In the distance the town was burning.

The forest trees waved their branches in fright.

But the little pine did not join in.

He was watching as two small children rushed towards him.

They were at the head of a long line of people leaving the town.

The young boy, Max, was being tugged along by his older sister, Lena.

They hid behind his trunk, away from the jet planes and metal monsters with their loud bangs.

Max and Lena began to sob.

Oh! How they missed their mum and dad who were back home, defending the town.

The little pine so wanted to help the children, but he didn't know how.

Then he had an idea.

He remembered the joyful sound of children playing in the forest. How they tossed pine cones up in the air like balls

... and raced
them
down
the
hill.

Gently he shook some of his own cones to the ground where Max and Lena accidentally kicked them.

Seeing how well they rolled, they began playing.

When the other trees saw how happy it made the children, they wanted to help too.

The kind trees and plants shared their fruit and nuts so the townspeople had more than enough to eat.

And there were plenty of sticks
for small campfires to warm
themselves by.

Soon all the children were running about playing games.

As darkness fell, more women and children arrived clutching small bags and teddy bears.

27

That night it rained on the poor children.

And the little pine found he wasn't wide
enough to keep the water off their heads.

He bent this way and that in the wind, but the
raindrops always seemed to find them.

Yet he never thought of giving up.

His small acts of kindness won the hearts of all the trees in the forest.

Seeing his struggle, the older trees interlocked their branches and formed a large, leafy canopy above the forest floor.

It gave the townspeople shelter from the worst of the wind and the rain. It also hid them from the jet planes to keep them safe.

The little tree shivered his pine needles to make a soft, whispering noise. It had a calming effect that helped the children sleep, in spite of the loud bangs.

One day there were fewer bangs.

And then they stopped altogether.

The townspeople left the forest and started to rebuild their homes from among the rubble.

Max and Lena went back to live with their mum and dad.

But they never forgot the little pine.

Every year they returned to give thanks and hung ribbons of remembrance on his now mighty branches.

Ingram Content Group UK Ltd.
Milton Keynes UK
UKHW050635040623
422791UK00003B/7